Alex, the Walking Accident

BOOKS for BOYS

IAN WHYBROW
ILLUSTRATED BY TONY ROSS

Hodder
Children's
Books

a division of Hodder Headline Limited

For Declan, grandson of my friend
David Mander, the inventor of the sideways
skateboard. We would often try them
out on the slope down to the promenade
at Westbrook. Sometimes we even made
it without bumping into the lamppost
at the bottom.

Text copyright © 2006 Ian Whybrow
Illustrations copyright © 2006 Tony Ross
First published in Great Britain in 2006
by Hodder Children's Books

The rights of Ian Whybrow and Tony Ross to be identified as the Author and
Illustrator of the Work have been asserted by them in accordance with the
Copyright, Designs and Patents Act 1988.

2

A Catalogue record for this book is available
from the British Library

ISBN 0 340 91111 5

Printed and bound in Great Britain by
Bookmarque Ltd, Croydon, Surrey

The paper and board used in this paperback by
Hodder Children's Books are natural recyclable products made from
wood grown in sustainable forests. The manufacturing processes conform
to the environmental regulations of the country of origin.

Hodder Children's Books
a division of Hodder Headline Limited
338 Euston Road
London NW1 3BH

Breakfast

Alex Dent and accidents seemed
to go together. That was why he
wasn't having much luck asking for
a new bike.

"No, you've already got a bike,"
said Mum. She was always in a
mood at breakfast. *Bang* went her
cup on to her saucer.

Alex didn't give up. "Yes, but I
need more gears."

Now it was Mr Dent's turn.

"You heard what your mum said. Forget it," he growled. "You know we haven't got the money to go buying you new bikes!"

There was a pile of letters beside his plate. He ripped one open. "Blast!" he roared. "There goes another job! I spent all that time designing office buildings for the Council and now they don't want them! They're giving the work to those idiots at Nettles and Partners! After all the effort I put in! They say my drawings are 'too modern'!"

"Don't worry, Charles, you're a *brilliant* architect," said Mrs Dent. "Things are bound to pick up soon." She tried to sound cheery but she didn't look it.

James, Alex's baby brother, was reaching down from his high chair towards Pud the cat. The cat was ignoring him. Alex meant to help. He tried to give Pud a little push towards James with his foot. Somehow he missed and trod on his tail.

"Yeeeeow!" went the cat and nearly scared the wits out of James.

"Waaah!" howled James.

"Alex!" shouted Mum and Dad together.

Alex kept going anyway. "All my friends say my bike's rubbish. It hasn't even got disc-brakes!"

He made a flapping movement with his hand to show how bad that was. Disaster.

Mr Dent's cornflakes were swimming in milk. On top he had plopped a great dollop of strawberry yoghurt. His spoon was in his bowl, with the handle resting on the side. So, when Alex's hand flapped out:

1. It knocked against the cornflakes box.

2. The box fell sideways and knocked over Dad's glass of orange juice.

3. The juice dived into Dad's lap – SPLOSH!

4. The glass fell at exactly the right angle to hit the handle of his spoon – TWANG!

5. Up went the spoon like a seesaw with a baby elephant on one end.

6. Suddenly soggy cornflakes and pink gunk started raining on everybody.

7. James threw his plate and hit Alex right on the ear – BONK!

"Axi Nutty Bye! Axi Nutty Bye!" screamed little James.

"Quite right! Alex is a *very* naughty boy!" agreed Mr Dent.

"Bad Axi!" scolded James. He always called Alex "Axi". He was only two. That was the nearest he could get to "Alex".

Mr and Mrs Dent thought that "Axi Dent" was just the right name for their son. He was a walking accident.

Gluggy's Little Outing

Things didn't get much better next day. Everybody was still miserable. James was in the bath, yelling as usual. This time it was because he was having his hair washed.

"Hush!" came Dad's voice up the stairs. "Daddy is trying to make an important phone call."

"*You* try hushing him," muttered Mrs Dent bitterly.

Mr Dent went back into his office

and closed the door behind him.
Alex opened it again and whacked
it into his dad's ankle. Not a good
moment, but normal for Axi Dent.

"Ouch!" shouted Mr Dent into
the phone. Somebody
had answered, so he
had to put on his
happy, busy voice.
"Hello! Chesney
Mould Property
Services? Can you
put me through to Mr Mould,
please?" He rubbed his ankle and
glared at his son.

"I'll just have a look on your
computer – see if I can find a bike
on eBay," said Alex.

"Go a-WAY!" hissed Dad.

"Go and play on your skateboard or something!" Suddenly, his voice went all charming again. "Ah, is that Chesney Mould? No, I didn't mean you. Sorry, I was talking to my son …"

"How can I go on my skateboard?" said Alex. "I haven't *got* a skateboard, and even if I had, there isn't a skateboard park round here.

And I can't go on my bike because everybody says it's rubbish …"

His dad clapped his hand over his spare ear. "Charles Dent here!" he said. He tried to get a laugh into his voice. "Hello, Chesney! I'm the chap you met the other day at the planning meeting. We said we'd have a little chat about building some houses on that land down by the bridge …?"

Alex was shocked. He jumped up from his dad's chair. The chair fell on his dad's toe. "They can't build on the land by the bridge!

That's where everybody
goes fishing!"

Mr Dent was
hopping about.
He was hopping
mad! "Will you hold
on one second,
Chesney?" He wrapped his hand
over the phone. "Alex! Please! This
is a very important call. Go a-WAY!
Go and help your mother with
James. I can't hear myself
THINK with him screaming!"

"How can I help?"
said Alex. "Nobody takes
any notice of me."

"Talk to James ... *Amuse*
him!" begged his dad. "Just stop
him screaming for five minutes!"

With that, he steered Alex out through his door with his foot and closed it firmly behind him.

"Easy for you to say," muttered Alex. "But what do you expect me to amuse him *with*?" He looked into the kitchen for an idea. Suddenly,

 his eye was taken by Gluggy – the goldfish – in his glass bowl on the worktop. "Aha!" said Alex and grabbed the bowl.

He hardly spilled a drop as he hurried up the stairs.

"Look, James! Look what Axi got!" he called. He swung his bottom against the bathroom door to open it.

"Gluggy come to kiss you better!"

James was startled. He froze like a shocked pink piglet. Bubbles crawled over his ears and eyes and slid down to his shoulders. Still, he didn't seem to notice.

All he could see was his big brother flying through the air. James had thrown his soap on to the floor. Now funny Axi had stepped on the soap! And here was a funny fish, too! A flying fish! Up flew the fishy, up in the air! Then the fishy did a dive and – *plink* –

he came swimming in the bath!

"Ha HA!" laughed James, much happier. Mummy screamed. Daddy rushed in. Then Daddy had to rush downstairs again to find something to catch Gluggy with. Then James pulled the plug out. Then Gluggy nearly swam down the plughole. Daddy was only just in time to catch him in a sieve!

What a good thing Gluggy was very brave and very good at holding his breath! Five minutes later he was safely back in his bowl.

Mum could breathe again, too. "Are you all right, Charles, dear?" she asked her husband.

"Delighted!" came his surprising reply. It turned out that he had managed to finish his conversation with the famous builder, Mr Mould. "And he's agreed to come over and have supper with us this evening!" Dad said with a smile. "He's going to look at my drawings and listen to my ideas about the way modern houses should be built. Oh, yes, and he's bringing his partner.

She's the one with the money. Just think, if we get on well, they might offer me some really important work!"

Mrs Dent looked worried. "B-but darling," she stuttered. "We haven't got anything nice to give them."

"What an opportunity!" exclaimed Dad dreamily. "There's room for at least fifty houses along the river. This could be my best job ever!"

"It's very good news, dear,"
said Mrs Dent. "But I wish you'd
given me a bit more time to prepare
supper."

"Don't worry, darling. Just make
your special chicken dish. That's
always a winner! I'll help clear up
and do the shopping. And Alex will
look after James … won't you, son!"

"Ouch, my
head!" said
Alex, giving his
bump a rub.
But no one
took any notice,
as usual. He was
stuck with James for
the whole afternoon.

The Sideways Skateboard

Alex didn't stick around in the house for long. There was too much dusting and hoovering and stuff going on.

In double-quick time, Mum had got the first part of her famous chicken dish ready. Pieces of chicken were soaking in some kind of juice. They would carry on soaking while Mum and Dad drove down to Sainsbury's to pick up

smelly candles,
paper serviettes,
nuts, stuffed
olives etc.

"Now listen to
me, Alexander,"
Mum said. He
knew he had to
expect trouble when she said his
whole name. He put on his *I'm
listening* face and his mum went on
in her MOODiest voice, "Tonight's
dinner is very important to me and

Dad. I intend to
make a *perfect* chicken
casserole and I don't
want anything to go
wrong, OK?"
"OK," whispered Alex.

"Now, you see that chicken in the dish on the table? It needs to go into the fridge at three o'clock. What time does it have to go into the fridge, Alexander?"

(Teeny voice.) "Three o'clock."

"Correct. You are to put the chicken into the fridge at three o'clock *exactly*. And if you forget, or if you let James even *touch* it, you are …"

(Teeny weeny voice) "… dead?" suggested Alex.

"That is not an expression I like," said Mrs Dent. "But it'll have to do for the moment."

Poor Alex. He always had problems stopping James from doing anything. So the safest thing, it seemed to Alex, was to take him out in his pushchair and give him a nice bumpy ride round the block. James liked bumpy rides.

Never mind strapping him in. No time for that, too tricky.

Babyminding was a pain, but at least it would give Alex a chance to try an experiment.

It was Dad talking about skateboards that gave him the idea.

"Just be careful!" his mum called after him as Alex slammed the front door. "Don't do anything silly. Look after Jamie properly. Make sure he doesn't pull his nappy off – we don't want any accidents. And *be back by three o'clock … you hear me!*"

Had she noticed that he was carrying a roller-skate and a short plank of wood? No, she was too busy worrying about her shopping list.

Normally, Alex would have popped along to one of his friends' houses – Matthew's or Dave's. But not today. Not with his baby brother tagging along.

So Alex was thinking, *Why not do something a bit more interesting than just walking? Why not push the pushchair along to the top of the High Street? There's a nice smooth bit of pavement there with a good slope. It runs all the way down to the post office. That will be perfect for trying out my idea for a do-it-yourself supersonic sideways skateboard!*

James sat quietly in his pushchair and watched Axi open up the roller-skate with his little spanner. He watched him lay the plank of wood across it, so that the skate was right in the middle.

It was good, the way he tightened the skate up to stop the plank falling off.

"You wait here," said Alex. He checked to see that the pushchair brake was on and turned the pushchair so that James could see what he was up to. "Now Jamie, watch Axi!"

He pointed the sideways skateboard down the slope and sat down carefully on it. He stretched out his arms so that his fingertips touched each end of the plank. Next, he lifted his feet off the ground and began to roll forward.

As he picked up speed, he began to drift towards the road. Whoops. Quickly he pressed down his left hand until the plank touched the flagstones. Too hard! He found himself spinning sharply. Then over and over he rolled – on to the grass.

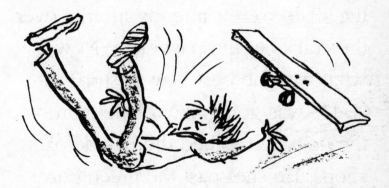

"Ha-HA!" yelled James. "Axi fall down!"

"Hang on!" puffed Alex, trotting back to his starting-point. "I see what I'm doing wrong." He lifted his feet up a bit higher this time and stretched his legs straight out in front of him. When the sideways skateboard started to drift in the wrong direction, he leant very gently the other way. Much better. Soon he was getting up a good speed and going quite straight. The wheels of the skate were clattering merrily over the cracks in the pavement. Now, what was the best way to stop?

He was going like a little train by the time he reached the parade of shops. He shot past the greengrocer and zoomed towards the post office. Still, he didn't panic. He made a wide V-shape with his legs and lowered his heels to the ground. That slowed him down a bit. Good! Then he jammed his hands down on the end of the board, first one side, then quickly the other. So with a lot of growling and grating and juddering, he managed to miss Mr Shaw. He had just stepped out of the post office with his Daily Mail rolled under his arm.

"What the …!" spluttered Mr Shaw.

"Hi, Mr Shaw! Don't worry!" said Alex.

There was a red pillar box outside the post office. Alex crashed into it. Ah, well, at least he'd stopped.

Standies

"Everything's under control," Alex said, trying to sound chirpy and rubbing the bits that hurt.

Not *quite* under control, perhaps, but after a few more goes, he got better. The trouble was, James was getting very restless. By the time Alex had zoomed down the slope three more times and raced back up again, James wanted to do sideways skateboarding, too. He began to cry.

Then he took his nappy off and
threw it at Alex.

Alex felt a bit stuck. His mum
had warned him about the nappy.
She would say it was all his fault
that James had taken it off. She'd be
even *more* angry if she thought he'd
made James cry. Luckily Alex had
another one of his
brilliant ideas. "Look,
Jamie!" he said, and
put the nappy on
his head. That did it.
No more tears!

"Sideways skate-
boarding is too hard for little boys,"
Alex explained. He pulled the
nappy snugly down round his ears
and looked through the leg-holes.

Good thing it was dry. "But wait, we'll do something else that you'll like …"

He moved the pushchair so that it was pointing down the slope and lined up the sideways skateboard behind it. As soon as he sat down on it, he realized that he was going to have a problem seeing where he was going. It wasn't just because of the nappy on his head. James and his pushchair were in his way. So there was nothing for it but to do a *standy*.

Of course, most people would have a little practice at standing on a sideways skateboard before trying a standy with a toddler in a pushchair. Not Alex. He felt that he had to

hurry up because James had got
bored. He'd already taken off
his nappy. He'd be climbing out of
his pushchair next! "Here we go,
then …" Alex said, gritting his teeth.

It was quite tricky balancing on
the board. You had to bend down
and let the brake off the pushchair
at the same time. But somehow,

Alex just about managed it without falling over. "Hold tight, Jamie!" he called. And off they went. James loved it. He screamed with delight.

Alex and James were just reaching their top speed when Alex saw the postman. He was on one knee, scooping letters out of the pillar box and into his sack. Alex thought,

I wonder how you stop a sideways skateboard from a standing position?

There was just time for an *uh-oh!* before he simply ... sat down. He was holding tight to the handle of the pushchair at the time. That was why, as he went backwards, he **flipped** James into the air, just like tossing a pancake.

"Oh dear, I should have strapped him in," he was thinking as he skidded and scraped along the pavement. It seemed ages before he came to a halt.

Luckily, the postman had his wits about him. In his spare time, he was wicket-keeper for his local cricket team. "Eye on the ball, Ernie!" he said to himself as the baby-pancake sailed towards him through the air. He ignored the sound of Alex crashing. He opened his hands as wide as they would go and – hup! – caught James, clean as a whistle. James never even touched the ground. "Howzat!" the postman cried. The people from the post office gave him a round of applause.

Jamie hadn't had so much fun since Gluggy had jumped into the bath with him. He laughed his little curly head off. All the people gathered round the boys and admired them and said how brave they were. And didn't the baby have a silly brother? Look at his funny hat! And his T-shirt ripped and his jeans all torn! And

what were their names and where
did they live? Would they like a
lift home?

"W-w-we're fine!" Alex stammered.
He guessed that his mum might not
want to hear about his sideways
skateboarding experiment. Not when
she was in a **mood**, anyway.

The thought of Mum's **mood**
made him look at his watch. Oh, no!
Five minutes to *chicken into the fridge or
die* time! He picked himself up,
popped James back into his
pushchair. This time he made sure
that he strapped him in. Finally
he handed James the sideways
skateboard to hold, before racing off
home as fast as he could hobble.

Crunchy Chicken

Three o'clock came and three
o'clock went and still Alex hadn't
made it home. It was a case of
more haste, less speed. James
loved it when Alex rushed him
along at a hobbling gallop.
"WHEEEEEEEE!" he squealed as
he was jiggled about.

The trouble was, other people
on the pavement weren't quite
so keen. They had to dive out of

the way into shop doorways or jump behind lampposts.

It was nearly ten past three when Alex made it through the door of his house. Thank goodness there was no sign of Mum or Dad. He unstrapped James and dashed to the kitchen.

Oh no! Pud was on the table with his fat face in the dish of chicken pieces.

"Scat! You horrible cat!" yelled Alex. He tugged the nappy off his head and hurled it at Pud.

James thought that was a very clever idea. He looked for something to throw, too. There was a sack of Kitty Litter behind the kitchen door. He knew it was the  stuff that went in Pud's toilet tray. He squatted down and came up with two handfuls of crumbly grey grit.

James let fly with both hands. The Kitty Litter came down like a thick grey hailstorm – WHAM! – right into the dish with the chicken.

Alex's face went the colour of the Kitty Litter. "Now I am definitely dead," he gulped.

Hurry!

In his little toddly way, James was rather touched by the look of horror on his big brother's face. He decided to be nice and leave him alone for a while. He went and watched the telly.

Alex didn't just lie down and wait to die. He took a deep breath and took action.

He grabbed a wooden spoon out of the kitchen drawer and tried to scoop some of the gungy Kitty Litter out from among the chicken pieces. Too slow! And too hard – what with all the little mushrooms and onions and chopped carrots. He gave the mixture a good stir and popped the dish into the fridge.

"Quick! Quick!" he whimpered to himself. "Now, clean nappies – where are they? Jamie! Come to Axi!" He knew that his mum would go mad if Jamie did a wee on the floor.

"Pleeeeeze!" Alex prayed.

"No more accidents today!"

Was that the car? He could always tell the car by the sound it made coming round the corner.

When Mr and Mrs Dent returned, fretting about crowds and traffic jams, they were amazed and delighted. How helpful Alex had been! There was James, sitting nicely on his potty. OK, he'd been bribed with chocolate ice cream. That was plain to see – he was covered in it. But never mind; the main thing was that

he was sitting quietly on his potty
and being very good.

Even more amazingly, the
table had been laid for four, very
carefully, with a beautiful tablecloth
covering it. And Alex had arranged
the best knives and

forks and the best glasses. He'd
done everything really neatly.

"Honestly, Alex," Dad said,
"that's brilliant!"

"Sorry if I was a bit harsh
earlier," said Mum.

Nightmare at Suppertime

Alex was delighted not to be invited to join the adults for supper. Still, he felt he ought to stick around and look useful, or he'd go mad with worry. Mum looked pleased, thanked him and said that he could hand out olives and dips and nibbles in the sitting room when the guests arrived.

By 7.30, James was in bed and the chicken casserole was simmering in the oven. "Please don't let them notice," prayed Alex.

Dad had a suit and tie on and he'd done something with his hair. Mum had her sparkly earrings on. "Fingers crossed, eh, Alex?" she said.

When she bent and kissed him, Alex *nearly* confessed everything. *Bing bong!* Saved by the doorbell!

Mould was a very good name for the man who came to supper. He was quite young, and very well dressed in a blue suit. He was large, with a big belly, and his trousers

were held up with broad yellow
braces. He had a strange, creaking
voice and terrible breath
like a damp cellar.
"Creepy," Alex thought.
  Mr Mould's business
partner, Miss Hannan
("the lady with the moneybags,
          haw! haw!") was nice.
          She had a lively,
          friendly smile.
        As he handed out
        nibbles, Alex found
        out one or two
things about the vistors. Mr Mould
liked talking about himself. Miss
Hannan hardly spoke at all.
  Mr Mould's big idea, Alex
gathered, was to make lots of "dosh"

for very little effort. He wanted
architects to design dozens of
houses to be built down by the
river. Then he would get builders to
build the houses for him. He would
get Miss Hannan to spend her
money on buying the land and
paying the builders. Then they
would sell the houses for millions.

Mr Mould raised his glass.
"Here's to dosh!" he drawled.

"Plenty for Miss Hannan, and plenty for you, Mr Dent … if you're my sort of architect. Now, what we're lookin' for is houses that *look* big without actually *being* big. Cram in as many as possible, yeah? That's the way to make people pay, haw haw!"

Mr Dent didn't look too happy about this. "Well, yes …" he said, "but people need space. They need light and air … Look, if I can just

show you some of my plans. I've got them on my laptop." He gave the laptop on the coffee table a little pat.

"Light and air!" scoffed Mr Mould. "You'll be talking about gardens next!"

"Well, I do happen to think that gardens are important – especially for the children," said Mr Dent.

"I thought you said you had *modern* ideas!" grunted Mould, tossing a big handful of nuts into his enormous mouth. "MMM, great, I'm starving! When do we get down to

the serious grub, Mrs D, eh? Haw haw! Anyway, look! As long as people have room to park a couple of cars, who cares about gardens?"

Miss Hannan looked
uncomfortable. She was about to say
something, but changed her mind.
There was an awkward silence.
Mr Dent poured more drinks.
Mrs Dent rushed off to see how the
casserole was coming along.

Alex felt that perhaps he ought
to say something. "Me and James
would go bonkers if we didn't have
a garden," he chirped.
"I mean, there aren't
many other places round
here where kids *can* play.
There isn't a skate
park or swings or
anything. And if you're going to
put houses down by the bridge,

we shan't even have a place to go fishing. It's great down by the river, you know. You get kingfishers and dippers and everything …"

Mr Mould made a face. "You know, sonny, when I was a kiddy, I was always in bed at this time of an evening …"

Dad took the hint. "My goodness! It *is* getting late. Alex – off you go now. You've been a great help, thank you."

Alex put on a show of going to his room. He popped his head round the kitchen door and said goodnight to his mum. After that, he headed for the stairs, stamping on every one to let the grown ups know that he was getting out of their way.

Then he lay down on the carpet on the upstairs landing and strained his ears. Normally he felt comforted by the homely, dusty smell of carpets, but now he felt ... doomed.

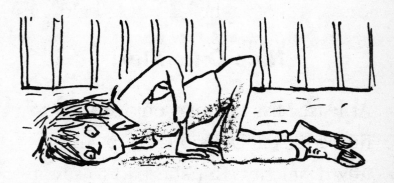

Why was he so unlucky? Wherever he went, accidents happened – to cornflakes, goldfish, sideways skateboards, pushchairs ... And now there was Kitty Litter in the casserole!

Something told Alex that at any moment he was going to be in DEEP trouble.

Nice One, Alex!

At least Miss Hannan enjoyed her first course. "Delicious soup!" Alex heard her say. But she had to say it above the noise of the increasingly angry conversation that his dad and Mr Mould were having. Dad was on about trees, how they make people feel good, the way they move, the sound of them.

"No way," rumbled Chesney Mould. "I don't want *nuffink* on that land that takes up space. Space costs us BIG dosh!"

"If you'd just let me show you the plan on my laptop," said Mr Dent, his voice rising.

"Darling, couldn't that wait at least till after we've eaten the casserole?" said Mrs Dent.

"Yeah! Let's eat!" interrupted Mr Mould. "I could eat a donkey! And never mind 'ladies first'! Pile it on my plate, Mrs D!"

Alex could imagine his mum's face. She hated bad manners. Still, she tried to keep the party going. Perhaps she was making a little joke to Miss Hannan while Mr Mould bellowed, "Don't be shy, Mrs D! More! More! What is it, chicken?

Lovely! Go on, another spoonful!
Mind if I start?"

"Tell you what, Charlie ..." said
Mr Mould through his food. Alex
winced. His dad hated being called
Charlie. There was a short pause
while Mr Mould shovelled more food
into his great mouth. You could
imagine it splattering over the table
as he spoke. "You're not one of them
Do-Gooders, are ya?
It'll be a waste of
time showing me
your plans if you
are! Because
Do-Gooders don't
believe in crammin' in
like I do, Haw! Haw! Yumm, mmm,
oh yeah ..."

56

Alex stuck his fingers into his ears and shut his eyes tight. He was expecting things to get noisy. But even he wasn't ready  for the explosion that followed.

"AAHHH! URRRGH! HELP! I'M CHOKING!"

"What!" yelled Mr Dent.

"I've been poisoned! BLEUGHH!"

Everyone started shouting at once. "What's the matter? What's going on?"

Suddenly, there was a sound of fists smashing down on the table like sledgehammers.

Then there were thumps, crashes, screams. The noise woke up James, so he showed everybody what *real* screaming sounds like.

Alex heard heavy feet pounding. Mr Mould was disgustingly sick. The front door slammed. An engine roared. Tyres screeched.

Alex had recently heard at school about King Charles having his head chopped off. He had wondered at the time what it must be like, having to kneel down and put your head on the chopping block. Now he knew.

When he peeped into the dining room with James, what they saw … was a TOTAL mess. The floor was

littered with broken plates and
dishes, glasses, knives and forks,
the supper, Mr Dent's laptop ... and
something else
that was truly
disgusting.

"Big sickie
on da floor!"
said James,
running over
and pointing
at it.

"Don't let
Jamie in here!" screamed Mum.
"There's broken glass everywhere!"
She picked him up and plonked
him in the hall for Alex to mind.

"What happened to Mr Mould?"
asked Alex.

"Gone!" said Dad, grimly.

"And he's not coming back, thank goodness!" cried Miss Hannan. "Honestly Mrs Dent, I had no idea that he could be so rude … such a PIG! Well, this evening has opened my eyes! I shall never do business with that dreadful man again. I'm not investing my money in any plan of his. I never want to see him again!"

"Call me Sarah," said Mum. She smiled and bent down to pick up a broken glass.

"I'm Nicola," smiled Miss Hannan. "Here, let me help you."

"There's no need," said Mrs Dent.

"Oh, but I'd like to," said Nicola
Hannan. "Really, this is too bad!
Chesney must have drunk far too
much of your wine. What a LOUT!
And your beautiful plates
smashed, look! Not to
mention your lovely
supper. And I was so
looking forward to
tasting your casserole,
Sarah! Such a shame!"

"Me too!" agreed Dad.
"Sarah, how about if you rustle us
up some cheese and some pudding?
Let me do the clearing up here."

"We'll both do it," said Miss
Hannan. "Then you can tell me
all about your plans, Mr Dent.

I'd *love* to see some of your designs, even if that greedy brute Chesney wasn't interested."

"Call me Charles, please," said Dad.

"Marvellous!" said the very charming Miss Hannan. "Oh, and Alex," she added, turning her smiling face towards him, "I'd really like to hear more of *your* suggestions for what to do with that land down by the river."

"Me?" said Alex. "You want to listen to *me*!"

"Certainly. The point you made about places for children to play – that was very important! I'm sure you'll have some *brilliant* suggestions for using that land by the river.

A skateboard park, you said.
And a conservation area for those
kingfishers and dippers. Surely
there's a way to design a really nice
housing estate and still have room
for trees and swings ... and ..."
She was getting really excited now
that she had a chance to speak.
"How about an adventure area for
bike riding? You do have a bike,
don't you, Alex?"

"Well, yes ..." said Alex. "But—"

"As a matter of fact," interrupted his dad, "his mother and I were thinking about getting him a new one. A lightweight off-roader, with proper suspension and plenty of gears!"

"And disc-brakes," added Alex.

"Disc-brakes! Yes! Disc-brakes are a must!" laughed Dad. "After all … safety first! We wouldn't want you having any accidents!"

"Ha HA!" laughed little James, just as if he knew what they were talking about.